BEDTIME for BABY SHARK

Doo Doo Doo Doo Doo Doo

Art by John John Bajet

■SCHOLASTIC

This edition published in the UK in 2019 by Scholastic Children's Books
Euston House, 24 Eversholt Street, London NW1 1DB
A division of Scholastic Ltd
www.scholastic.co.uk
London – New York – Toronto – Sydney – Auckland – Mexico City – New Delhi – Hong Kong

First published in 2019 by Cartwheel Books, an imprint of Scholastic Inc., U.S.A.
Copyright © Scholastic Inc., 2018
Adapted from the song, "Baby Shark".

ISBN 978 140719 769 2
All rights reserved.
Printed in Italy

1 3 5 7 9 8 6 4 2

Deep in the ocean,
Late late at night
All the creatures were sleeping
Snuggled up tight.

The minnows were snoozing
And the whales snored deep.
But one baby shark . . .
Would NOT go to sleep.

Brush your teeth, doo doo doo doo doo doo.
Brush your teeth, doo doo doo doo doo doo.

Brush your teeth, doo doo doo doo doo doo.
BRUSH YOUR TEETH!

Take a bath, doo doo doo doo doo doo.
Take a bath, doo doo doo doo doo doo.

Take a bath, doo doo doo doo doo doo.
TAKE A BATH!

Jammies on, doo doo doo doo doo doo.
Jammies on, doo doo doo doo doo doo.

Jammies on, doo doo doo doo doo doo doo.

JAMMIES ON!

Read a book, doo doo doo doo doo doo.
Read a book, doo doo doo doo doo doo doo.

Read a book, doo doo doo doo doo doo.
READ A BOOK!

Night-light on, doo doo doo doo doo doo.
Night-light on, doo doo doo doo doo doo.

Night-light on, doo doo doo doo doo doo doo.

NIGHT-LIGHT ON!

Toss and turn, doo doo doo doo doo doo.
Toss and turn, doo doo doo doo doo doo.

Toss and turn, doo doo doo doo doo doo doo.

TOSS AND TURN!

Run and hide, doo doo doo doo doo doo.
Run and hide, doo doo doo doo doo doo doo.

Run and hide, doo doo doo doo doo doo.
RUN AND HIDE!

No more tricks, doo doo doo doo doo doo.
No more tricks, doo doo doo doo doo doo doo.

No more tricks, doo doo doo doo doo doo. **NO MORE TRICKS!**

All tucked in, doo doo doo doo doo doo.
All tucked in, doo doo doo doo doo doo.

All tucked in, doo doo doo doo doo doo.
ALL TUCKED IN!

Off to sleep, doo doo doo doo doo doo.
Off to sleep, doo doo doo doo doo doo.

BABY SHARK BEDTIME DANCE!

BRUSH YOUR TEETH!

Move hand up and down in front of your mouth like a toothbrush.

TAKE A BATH!

Wave a hand behind your head like a scrub brush.

JAMMIES ON!

Squat, then stand up, pulling on invisible pyjamas.

READ A BOOK!

Unfold hands like a book.

NIGHT-LIGHT ON!

Pull on an imaginary chain.

TOSS AND TURN!

Hold hands beside head, then twist and turn.

RUN AND HIDE!

Run in place.

NO MORE TRICKS!

Wag your finger back and forth.

ALL TUCKED IN!

Cross arms across chest and sway.

OFF TO SLEEP!

Put hands together under your head.